Jesus LOVES <u>You</u>!

Erik Tanouske

Book 1

# We're Going to Heaven!

## By Rick Tancreto
### Art by Mary Bausman

Little Saints Press
Piney Point, Maryland

www.LittleSaintsPress.com

# Dedication

For my children,
Rick and Diane,
and their precious families.
—Pops

With thanks to my mother and dad, my husband, Cal, and my dear family
for continuing to put crayons in my hands.
And a special thanks to God for guiding each creative stroke.
—M.B.

This book was written by Rick Tancreto (Rick@LittleSaintsPress.com); cowritten by Joyann Browne;
edited by Lori Peckham; designed by square1studio; illustrated by Mary Bausman © 2017 www.marybausman.com. Children advisers: Dominick and Danny Caparotti; Reef Peckham; Connor, Ellie, Luke, Joy, and Lucy Senechal; Nicholas and Karalyn Ashenfelter.

Tancreto, Rick.
We're going to heaven! / by Rick Tancreto ; art by Mary Bausman.
p. cm. — (Hang on to Jesus! adventures ; bk. 1)
SUMMARY: Nine-year-old Ricky, his younger sister, Dee Dee, and their dog, Maxie, go on an imaginary adventure to heaven with Jesus as their guide.
Audience: Ages 5-9.

LCCN 2011931446
ISBN-13: 978-1-936831-00-5
ISBN-10: 1-936831-00-7

1. Heaven—Juvenile fiction. 2. Jesus Christ—
Juvenile fiction. [1. Heaven—Fiction. 2. Jesus Christ—
Fiction.] Bausman, Mary, ill. II. Title.
III. Series: Tancreto, Rick. Hang on the Jesus! adventures ; bk. 1.

PZ7.T161355Wer 2011 [E]
QBI11-600153

ISBN 978-1-936831-00-5

"Jesus said,
'Let the little children come to me.
Don't stop them, because the kingdom
of heaven belongs to people who
are like these children.'"

Matthew 19:14

**The** spring rain shower stopped suddenly, giving way to a brilliant sun peeking through the few remaining clouds.

Dee Dee could hardly wait to go back outside and enjoy her favorite activity—swinging. Bouncing down the back porch steps, she raced toward the big oak tree and wiped the raindrops off the wooden seat. "Nice and dry," she concluded, as she hopped up onto the swing and began pumping her feet.

The sky seemed to draw closer and closer with each pump. "I wonder what it's like up there . . . beyond the clouds and the sun," Dee Dee pondered out loud. "I wonder what it's like *way* up there . . . in heaven."

"Think only about the things in heaven,

Then, pumping as hard as she could, Dee Dee shouted, "I want to go so high that I can touch heaven!"

Ricky listened quietly from the porch. *So, my sister wants to touch heaven*, he thought to himself. *Maybe I can help her.*

Sneaking up behind Dee Dee, he positioned himself to push her with all of his might. "Did you mean *this* high?" he snickered.

**not the things on earth."** Colossians 3:2

"Ahhhhh!" cried out Dee Dee, as she rocketed off the swing and through the air.

Ricky moved aside as his sister tumbled to the ground.

Beginning to cry, she wailed, "You did that on purpose!"

Ricky chuckled. "I was just trying to help you get up to heaven!"

"We are citizens of heaven. And we can hardly wait for a Savior

"Why are you so mean?" whimpered Dee Dee. "Don't you know that mean brothers won't get into heaven?"

"What do *you* know about what it takes to get into heaven?" Ricky shot back.

As Dee Dee brushed herself off, she saw something out of the corner of her eye. She couldn't believe what she was seeing, so she rubbed her teary eyes. Then she rubbed them again. Jesus was walking toward them!

"Ricky," she whispered, "do you see who I see? It's . . . it's . . . *Jesus*. You know, from the Bible."

Ricky's jaw dropped open.

As Jesus came closer, He smiled.

**from there. He is the Lord Jesus Christ."** Philippians 3:20 (NiRV)

"Hi, Dee Dee; hi, Ricky," Jesus greeted them. "I'm glad you recognized Me."

Dee Dee's heart jumped. Wiping away the last remaining tear, she stammered, "J-Jesus! I can't believe You're here—with us! But *why* are You here? And how'd You get here? Did You come down from heaven? I bet You could tell us all about heaven! Will You? Will You tell us what heaven is like?"

Jesus smiled again. "You are filled with great questions, Dee Dee. And yes, I will tell you all about heaven . . . or I could take you and Ricky on an adventure into heaven to see what it will be like."

"No kidding?" Ricky responded, his eyes as big as bottle caps.

Jesus raised His hand, and a golden stairway appeared in front of them. It reached far into the sky, disappearing into the clouds.

"Wow!" yelled Dee Dee. "We *are* going on a journey into heaven!"

5

"Jesus answered, 'I am the way . . . The only

Ricky turned to Jesus. "Only You can get us into heaven! Thank You, Lord."

Jesus put His arm around Ricky. "Heaven awaits everyone who believes in Me."

Maxie gazed steadily at Jesus, wagging her tail. "Yes, Maxie," laughed Jesus, "you can come too."

**way to the Father is through me.'"** John 14:6

"Where I'm taking you," Jesus explained,
"is where I live. And it's the place I'm
preparing for those children and grown-
ups who believe in Me."

"We can't wait to see what You've
planned for us!" exclaimed Ricky,
following Jesus onto the stairway.

"You always show me the path that leads to life. You will fill me with joy when I am

"What are we going to see, Jesus?" Dee Dee shouted, as she scrambled up the stairway. "Are we going to see animals? Is there a zoo?"

"What about trees?" asked Ricky. "Are there going to be trees so I can build a huge tree house like the one in my backyard? Will I have my own room?"

"And what about playing?" Dee Dee hollered down. "Can I play up in heaven?"

Jesus laughed. "So many questions! And I love questions."

"Oh, good," Ricky sighed, as he continued with another question. "So, Jesus, what do You think will be the first thing we'll see in heaven?"

"You'll want to see a special book, called the Book of Life."

"What makes it special?" Dee Dee asked.

"It contains the names of those who will enter into heaven."

Both Ricky and Dee Dee stopped climbing and stared at each other. "*Really?*" Dee Dee said in awe. "Can we see if our names are in the book?

"Sure," answered Jesus.

Glancing at Ricky, she added, "But I'm very *skeptical* about seeing my brother's name there." Dee Dee liked to use big words.

Jesus smiled. "You'd be surprised by whose names are in the Book of Life. Come, children, we're almost there."

with you. You will give me endless pleasures at your right hand." Psalm 16:11 (NiRV)

"I will never erase their names from the Book of Life, but I will announce

As they approached the special book, Dee Dee stood on her tiptoes to try to reach it. But she couldn't. Then she felt the hands of Jesus lift her up.

"Hmmm," said Dee Dee, "my name's not on this page." She began flipping through the book. "Not here either . . . Not on this page . . . Not here . . . or here . . . Nothing here . . ."

Ricky shuffled his feet, anxious to see if *his* name was in the book.

"Nope," cried Dee Dee, "not on this page . . . or this one . . . or this one . . ."

Jesus placed His hand on Dee Dee's and guided it to a page near the middle of the Book of Life. "Look!" Dee Dee called out suddenly. "My name *is* here! And guess what, Ricky? So is yours! That means we can enter heaven. Oh, Jesus, *now* You can show us everything!"

"Phew." Ricky breathed a sigh of relief.

Placing Dee Dee back on her feet, Jesus smiled. "Let's go see what heaven is like."

As they walked toward a gate fashioned out of a single giant pearl, the children could hardly believe what was happening. They were about to journey into heaven.

**before my Father and his angels that they are mine."** Revelation 3:5 (NLT)

"No eye has seen, no ear has heard, and no mind has imagined what

Passing through the gate, the children felt as though they were stepping into another world. "Whoa!" uttered Dee Dee, as she paused to take in some of heaven's glory.

"Look all around you," Jesus directed the children. "Behold the dazzling brightness everywhere. Take notice of the streets made of gold. Look out on the spectacular gardens and crystal river. Listen to the singing and the musical instruments being played. Gaze at the children playing together and the people eating the finest food one could imagine. Cast your eyes upon the people worshipping and praising My Father."

"God the Father lives here too?" interjected Ricky.

"Yes," said Jesus, "along with all of the people from the Bible who believe in Me."

"Would that include Noah and Moses?" asked Dee Dee.

Jesus nodded. "It also includes all of your friends and family members who believe in Me."

"This is so much more than I ever imagined!" concluded Ricky. "I'm blown away!"

*But I wonder if this is as far as we can go in heaven*, Dee Dee said to herself. *I'd sure love to see lots more of this paradise.*

Knowing Dee Dee's thoughts, Jesus said, "Come, let's go explore heaven."

**God has prepared for those who love him."** 1 Corinthians 2:9 (NLT)

As the adventure began, Ricky noticed something he hadn't ever seen before. "Who are they?" he asked.

"Those are angels, silly!" answered Dee Dee.

"Well, sis," barked Ricky, with his hands on his hips, "it's not like I hang out with angels back home."

"Be careful. Don't think these little children are not important. I tell

Jesus laughed. "You may not hang out with angels, Ricky, but they hang out with you."

"For real?" Ricky said with a surprised look on his face. "I've never seen one."

"That's because on earth they're invisible most of the time," said Jesus. "But they're always near you, watching over you when you're at school, at play, and even asleep."

"Oh, Ricky, isn't that *heartening!*" Dee Dee said excitedly.

Ricky rolled his eyes, wondering where his sister had heard that big word before.

"*Heartening!*" Dee Dee repeated.

Just as Ricky was going to put his hands on his hips again, he spotted something else unusual. "What's that big chair for, Lord?"

"That's My throne. It's where I reward people for the things they did while on earth."

Filled with excitement, Dee Dee cried out, "Lord, will I be receiving any rewards?"

Jesus pointed toward His throne. "Let's find out!"

14

**you that these children have angels in heaven."** Matthew 18:10 (ERV)

As Jesus took His rightful place on His throne, He invited
Dee Dee to come forward and receive one of her rewards.
Her knees almost buckled as she walked toward the throne.

Placing a crown on her head, Jesus said, "This is your
reward for the many good deeds you performed, including
the time you comforted your friend, Lori, when her cat was
hit by a car."

Dee Dee was speechless. She had just been crowned by
Jesus for doing good in His eyes.

**"The Son of Man is going to come in his Father's glory with his angels, and then he will
reward each person according to what they have done."** Matthew 16:27 (NIV)

Jesus then motioned for Ricky to step forward. His knees were also shaking.

"Ricky," Jesus said as He placed a crown on his head, "this is your reward for the many good deeds you performed, including the time you broke up a fight between two boys on the school playground."

"Thank You, Lord," was all Ricky could utter. He was also speechless.

Jesus continued, "I have even more good news. There's something else you'll wear with your crowns."

**"Now, a crown is being held for me—a crown for being right with God."** 2 Timothy 4:8

Jesus stood up and asked Ricky to come stand beside Him. "In heaven, you're clothed in a new body, a heavenly body," Jesus explained as He put a robe on him.

"Whoa! I feel like a new person!" Ricky said, as he inspected his new heavenly body. "Why do I feel so different?"

"Down on earth, bodies get sick and injured . . . like when you had the flu, Ricky, and when you fell off the swing, Dee Dee. Here in heaven, you'll never get sick, or hurt, or be in pain, or feel sadness."

Next, Jesus invited Dee Dee to come and be clothed in her new body. "Dee Dee, on earth bodies will wear out and die," He said. "But in heaven your new bodies will last forever."

Jesus smiled as He saw the expression on the children's faces.

"Did you hear that, Ricky?" said Dee Dee. "You'll never die when you're in heaven because you have a perfect body!"

"That's amazing!" Ricky realized.

**"This body that dies must clothe itself with something that will never die."**
1 Corinthians 15:53 (ERV)

"But if we're going to live in heaven forever," Dee Dee chimed back in, "we'll need a place to stay . . . won't we, Lord?"

"I'm glad you asked that, because I have a special place ready for you," Jesus answered. "Come, let Me show it to you."

As they began walking, Ricky leaned toward his sister and said gleefully, "Because our names are in the *special* book, we have a *special* place to stay in heaven! Isn't that *special?*"

Dee Dee looked up at Jesus. "Sounds like Ricky finally discovered one of his own big words."

Jesus and Ricky laughed.

**"He will wipe away every tear from their eyes, and there will be no more death, sadness, crying, or pain."** Revelation 21:4

On their journey to the children's special place, Jesus brought them through one of heaven's lush meadows. "Hey, Ricky," said Dee Dee, with a puzzled look on her face, "do you notice anything *peculiar* about these animals?"

Ricky shrugged his shoulders. "I don't even know what your big word means, so how could I notice anything *peculiar*?"

"Do you notice anything unusual?" she clarified. "Anything strange?"

"You mean besides you?" Ricky laughed until his sides hurt.

"No, silly! The animals . . . they're all playing and snuggling together."

"Then wolves will live in peace with lambs, and leopards will lie down to rest with them. Cows and bears will eat together in peace. Their young will lie

"Hey, you're right! What's up with that?"

"Lord," asked Dee Dee, "why is the bear eating *with* the cow . . . and not *eating* the cow?"

"In heaven, all the animals are gentle and don't hurt one another," Jesus explained. "Go ahead, you can pet them."

Dee Dee stroked the lion's mane. "Cool! Now it's your turn, Ricky!"

At first, Ricky thought he'd pet the wolf, but then he chose to pet the lamb instead . . . the one that was asleep.

Dee Dee laughed. "Baaaaaaaa!"

Trying to change the subject, Ricky asked Jesus, "Are we there yet?"

Jesus grinned. "Almost. Follow Me."

**goats. Calves, lions, and young bulls will eat together, and a little child will lead down to rest together. Lions will eat hay as oxen do."** Isaiah 11:6, 7

As they approached an enormous mansion nestled high up on a hill, Ricky asked, "Who lives there, Lord?"

"You do."

"Really?" asked Dee Dee.

"This is My Father's house," Jesus explained, "and inside is the place I've prepared for you."

"I just love heaven!" Dee Dee yelled as loud as she could.

Jesus smiled and invited the children inside the mansion to see their special place.

**"There are many rooms in my Father's house; I would not tell you this if**

"Oh, Jesus!" Dee Dee called out, trembling with excitement. "This is . . . it's *exquisite*!" She tried to take in all the details around her. "And You did all of this for us? Thank You, Lord!"

"Wow!" yelled Ricky, as he scanned his new surroundings. "This is a million times nicer than anything back home. I'm so ready to move in!"

As Dee Dee was just about to sit down next to her brother, she heard Jesus' name being called from outside the mansion. "What's going on?" she inquired.

"Come," said Jesus, "let's go see."

it were not true. I am going there to prepare a place for you." John 14:2

"Come join us, Jesus!" the children playing near the crystal river cried out.

As Jesus joined in, He motioned for Ricky and Dee Dee to join in too.

"This is so much fun!" bellowed Dee Dee, her voice trailing off as she ran along the river's edge.

"I'm having a blast!" Ricky yelled as he splashed under the waterfall with some of his new friends.

"After I go and prepare a place for you, I will come back and take

Everyone was having
the time of their life. The
excitement went on for hours.

"Lord," said Ricky, "we're having the best
time being with You and the other kids. Is this
how we'll spend some of our time in heaven?"

Jesus nodded. "We'll be best friends forever!"

"I can't wait, Lord!" Dee Dee said with a smile. "Would You tell us how we
can be with You forever, in heaven?"

"Sure, but now it's time for Me to return you to your earthly home. We can
talk about it on the way."

you to be with me so that you may be where I am." John 14:3

On their journey, Dee Dee couldn't take her eyes off Jesus. "Thank You for showing us what heaven will be like," she said. "I'd do anything to be there someday."

"Yeah!" exclaimed Ricky. "There's nothing that can keep me from going to heaven. It's wonderful!"

"Come, children," Jesus said, "sit down next to Me."

As the children drew near to Jesus, He said, "I'd like nothing more than for you to join Me in heaven someday."

Ricky and Dee Dee smiled at each other. Ricky added a thumbs-up.

"But there's just one problem," explained Jesus, "and it's a big one."

"Brothers, listen! We are here to proclaim that through this man Jesus there is forgiveness

The children's smiles faded away. "What's that, Lord?" asked Dee Dee.

"Sin."

"What's sin?" inquired Ricky.

Dee Dee jumped in with the answer. "It's when a person does what is wrong . . . like when you pushed me off the swing!"

Jesus continued, "And it's your sin that can keep you out of heaven."

"OK, then I'll just have to be extra good," confessed Ricky. "Yeah . . . there'll be no more pushing you off the swing from now on, sis. That's the kind of *being good* I'm capable of!"

"And I'll do a bunch of good deeds for my family and friends," added Dee Dee. "That should get me in."

"Being good and doing good won't get you into heaven," Jesus explained.

Ricky looked puzzled. "Then what will, Lord?"

"Everyone sins, and that means they need to be forgiven for their sins before they can enter into heaven. So I came to earth to pay the penalty for sin."

"What was the penalty, Lord?" asked Dee Dee.

"I died on a cross for the forgiveness of sin. Those who accept My gift of forgiveness and who believe in Me will have their sins forgiven."

The children stared at each other in amazement. They began to realize the depth of Jesus' love.

A few silent moments passed before Ricky belted out, "I told you Jesus was the only one who could get us into heaven!"

"I want to go to heaven someday, Lord," pleaded Dee Dee, "so I want to know more about You . . . and forgiveness . . . and sin . . . and heaven . . . and believing in You . . . and the cross. . ."

Jesus stood up and guided the children down the next few golden steps. "How about if I show you where to learn more about everything we've seen and talked about on our journey?"

They both agreed eagerly.

26

for your sins. Everyone who believes in him is made right in God's sight." Acts 13:38, 39 (NLT)

Back in Ricky's room, Jesus took the Bible from the nightstand and opened it. "All of the important things you'll ever need to know are right here in your Bible."

"Including about You, Jesus?" asked Dee Dee. "And heaven?"

"Yes, the Bible is how I get to talk to you, and prayer is how you get to talk to Me."

"I'll read the Bible every day, Jesus!" promised Ricky.

Looking up into Jesus' eyes, Dee Dee smiled and said, "We'll pray every day too."

As Maxie wagged her tail, it brushed across Ricky's face, tickling him and making him laugh . . .

**"Everything in the Scriptures is God's Word. All of it is useful for teaching and helping**

**Ricky felt something** furry brush across his face. "What was that?" he mumbled. "Oh, it's just Maxie's tail."

He opened his sleepy eyes and rubbed them. Then he rubbed them again. Surprised, he realized that he and Maxie were alone in his room.

"Ricky, are you awake?" Dee Dee bounded down the hallway and into his room. Out of breath, she managed to say, "I just had the most *incredible* dream! I was up in heaven with Jesus, and you were there too. Did you hear me? Heaven! We were up in heaven!"

Ricky smiled. "Yeah, I know. I think I had the same dream. And it was incredible." He pulled the covers up under his chin and smiled again.

# Heaven sounds wonderful!
## How does a person get there?

**H**eaven is wonderful—more wonderful than pictures or words could ever describe. What makes it so perfect? Jesus lives there! And in the Bible, He tells us exactly how to get there.

**"No eye has ever seen or no ear has ever heard or no mind has ever thought of the wonderful things God has made ready for those who love Him."** 1 Corinthians 2:9 (NLV)

Because heaven is perfect, the smallest trace of sin cannot enter. Sadly, we've all sinned, and that means we all have a big problem!

**"For all have sinned."** Romans 3:23 (NLT)

While we were still sinners, Jesus did something amazing. He came down from heaven to rescue us! He died on a cross to pay the penalty for our sin—something we could not do for ourselves. His death took away our sin. And He did something else amazing. He rose from the grave and forty days later went back to heaven. So now anyone who believes in what Jesus did for them will go to heaven too!

**"Anyone who believes in God's Son has eternal life."** John 3:36 (NLT)

Do you believe that Jesus died for you? If so, He invites you to pray to Him:

Dear Jesus,

    I want to go to heaven one day, but I know that because of my sin I am without hope of getting into heaven on my own.

    I believe that You came down from heaven to rescue me from my sin.

    Thank You, Jesus, for willingly going to the cross to pay the penalty for my sins.

    I am sorry for my sins—truly sorry. Please forgive me for the wrong things I've done.

    I believe that You rose from the grave and You're in heaven, and someday You'll welcome me there.

    Amen.

If you prayed this prayer to Jesus and believed what you said to Him, you can be certain that someday He will welcome you to your new eternal home—heaven!

**"The Lord . . . will bring me safely to his heavenly kingdom."** 2 Timothy 4:18 (NIV)